DRAGON CHILD

To Alex, a true DragonChild.

First published 2013 by A & C Black,
an imprint of Bloomsbury Publishing Plc
50 Bedford Square
London WC1B 3DP

www.bloomsbury.com

Copyright © 2013 A & C Black
Text copyright © 2013 Gill Vickery
Illustrations copyright © 2013 Mike Love

ISBN 978-1-4081-8825-5

A CIP catalogue for this book is available from the British Library.

DRAGON CHILD

The Topaz Quest

GILL VICKERY

Illustrated by
MIKE LOVE

A & C BLACK
AN IMPRINT OF BLOOMSBURY
LONDON NEW DELHI NEW YORK SYDNEY

Northern Sea

Eastern Sea

Fellhof

East Eldkeiler Mts

Drakelow Mts

Kulafoss

Drangur

Holmurholt

Askarlend

Roornhof

Southern Sea

The Story So Far...

Tulay was a peaceful land until a family of High Witches stole the DragonQueen's necklace set with six jewels of power. The High Witches divided the jewels between them and used their power to drive the dragons away.

In revenge, a dragon kidnapped the youngest witch's child, a girl called Tia. Raised by dragons, Tia wants to prove she is a true DragonChild by recovering the jewels and returning them to the DragonQueen. Her DragonBrother, Finn, is with her on the quest.

Tia and Finn first stole back the emerald, which grants the power to talk to animals, from High Witch Malindra who ruled the town of Drangur. Next they went to Kulafoss and stole the opal from High Witch Yordis. The opal lets its possessor change into whatever creature they wish.

Now they are on their way to recover the topaz which controls the weather. High Witch Luona has it and she lives in the town of Stoplar.

Chapter One

The Ice Storm

Tia stared in horror at the shrieking ice-storm blocking the pass into Stoplar. She had walked a long way to reach the town and its lands hidden deep in the forbidding Eldkeiler Mountains and now the way was barred by the storm. Raging wind threw splinters of ice like broken sword blades against the towering, frost-coated sides of the pass.

The screaming storm made it impossible to talk to her friends so she pointed to a grove of stunted trees huddling by the river flowing past the foot of the mountainside. The little dragon and the jackdaw nodded in understanding and flew into the thicket.

Tia stumbled after them over the rocky ground, the bitter wind pushing her along like a cold hand. 'It's not fair,' she grumbled. 'If they'd let me be a falcon again I could move as fast as they can.'

When she reached the trees she found that her DragonBrother, Finn, had started a campfire and pushed a mossy log close to it. She sat on it and warmed her hands at the fire.

'DragonTeacher warned us that High Witch Luona uses the topaz to control the weather and rule Stoplar, but he didn't tell us about that ice-storm,' Finn said. He nudged Tia anxiously with his nose. 'We need to find another way to get you in.'

Tia patted him. 'Don't worry so much, Finn.' She turned to the jackdaw perched on a rock next to her. 'As we can't use the pass, what do you think we should do, Loki?'

'I think I'm going to find myself some food,' he said, and flew off.

Tia realised she was hungry too and rummaged in her bag. 'I've only got stale bread and a lump of cheese.' She skewered the food on a stick and toasted it over the flames.

When she'd finished, she licked melted cheese off her fingers. 'That was good but I wish I'd brought some sweet pies from Kulafoss before we left.'

'You were too busy turning yourself into a bird and showing off,' Finn said.

Tia touched a large opal set into a collar round her neck. She'd used the jewel to turn into a falcon.

'Don't change now!' Finn said.

'I'm not going to. I was just thinking, I could become a falcon again and fly over the mountains.'

Little puffs of smoke burst from Finn's nostrils. 'It's far too high for a small bird. And you mustn't use the opal in Stoplar – what if you were seen changing?'

'I wouldn't be,' Tia said indignantly. 'But I won't use it.'

Leaves rustled above their heads and Loki flew down.

'You're talking about the opal aren't you?' he said.

Tia nodded. Though Loki didn't understand Finn Tia could speak to the jackdaw because she kept the magic emerald with her. It gave her the power to speak to any animal.

'After you'd been a bird in Kulafoss,' Loki said, 'you wanted to be one all the time. If you change into a falcon to get into Stoplar you won't be able to resist doing it again once you're there. Remember how Yordis ended up more like a bear than a woman? It was because she couldn't stop using the opal, and you won't be able to either.'

Her friends didn't understand, Tia thought. It wasn't turning into another creature that was tempting – it was being able to fly!

'What do you two think I should do, then?' she asked.

'I'll disguise myself and carry you over the mountains,' Finn said.

Tia flung her arms round the little dragon's muzzle. 'No! That's too dangerous. I know you've practised camouflaging yourself but if you make a mistake, even for a second, the spell will catch you.'

She knew the power of the spell cast by the High Witches around each of the lands of the six towns. The dragon who'd snatched her from her parents when she was very small had been caught up in it and tossed through the air like a rag. He'd dropped her and only just managed to scoop her up again before she crashed to the ground. She shivered at the memory and hugged her DragonBrother even harder. He shook her off.

'It'll be quite safe,' he insisted. 'I'm very good at disguising myself now.'

It was true. Finn could change his colour to match his surroundings perfectly. Not even the spell could 'see' him when he did that.

Finn stubbornly stuck to his plan and finally Tia agreed.

'All right, that's what we'll do. When shall we go into Stoplar?'

'At night time – it's easy to make myself the colour of shadows,' Finn said.

Tia looked up at the dusky sky. 'Shall we spy out the lie of the land by daylight first, to find the best way in?'

Her friends agreed and they settled down for the night.

By the time the stars were out Finn and Loki were sound asleep but Tia was wide awake. Thoughts of flying drifted through her mind: how she hadn't been afraid high in the sky and how the wind whistled and blew around her; how warm drafts of air lifted her up as easily as a dry leaf and how much she could see looking down from the sky.

She saw herself as a dragon. She couldn't help it; it was what she wanted more than anything else in the world. When she was very little she'd used a piece of old rope as a tail and flapped her arms pretending they were wings. The dragonets had laughed at her, especially the bully, Torkil. 'You'll never be a dragon – witch brat!' he'd jeered.

Tia snuggled closer to the comfort of her DragonBrother's warm, soft hide.

When she was in Kulafoss she'd discovered that Torkil was right – she was a witch child. She could raise fire and see spells sparkling in the air. It wasn't fair! She didn't want to be a witch – she wanted to be a dragon.

She touched the opal lightly and made up her mind. She'd sneak away before dawn while Finn and Loki were still asleep and turn herself into a dragon. They would never know because she *wouldn't* start using the opal all the time as they feared. She could stop whenever she wanted. And anyway, it was all right for them to talk – they could fly.

Chapter Two

DragonChild

Tia crept out of the clump of trees, taking care not to wake her friends, and scrambled quickly up the lower slopes of the mountain to a big, flat-topped shelf of rock. It was harder to reach than she'd thought and by the time she clambered onto it the moon had disappeared and a few rays of amber and gold light were spreading over the horizon.

She walked as close to the edge of the big rock as she dared and looked down. At once her head swam and she began to tremble and sweat. Being a falcon hadn't got rid of her fear of heights: human-Tia was just as afraid as ever.

She stumbled backwards and leaned against the wall of the mountain where she waited until the trembling steadied and her heart stopped pounding like horses' hooves.

As soon as she was calm she touched the opal and thought of dragons. Images flashed through her mind – red, blue and green dragons, roaring, flying, snorting smoke and breathing fire. In an instant she changed. Her skin became scaly, her nails grew into claws and wings sprouted from her back. She was a dragon.

She roared in excitement and smoke poured from her nostrils, fire from her mouth. It was hot! She hiccupped and the smoke went backwards into her throat, making her cough until her eyes ran.

When she could breathe properly again she strode towards the edge of the rock. It didn't seem at all strange to be walking on four limbs. And when she looked down to the land below, her dragon self wasn't in the least bit afraid.

She shook out her wings and flapped them gently. She felt a press of air beneath them lift her slightly. At that moment the sun slid over the horizon and bathed her in full sunlight. It glittered off her scaly hide and to her astonishment she saw that she was a golden-red colour. She'd turned to the colour of human-Tia's hair. Without another thought, she dived from the rock and soared into the sky.

Being a dragon was wonderful. She slipped through the air as easily as a fish slips through water.

She dived and twirled and swooped. She flew fast, she flew slowly. She flew upside down and ran into a skein of geese making its way towards the far-away lakes of Holmurholt. They honked in alarm and their V-shape formation broke up.

'I'm sorry,' Tia called to them but they took no notice, just re-formed and flapped away.

Stupid geese, Tia thought a bit guiltily. She really should've looked where she was going. And that reminded her; she had a job to do – finding the best way over the mountains and into Stoplar. She wheeled round and found herself flying dangerously close to the spell she could see shimmering like spider silk in the sun. She thought of the warning chant all dragons knew by heart:

If the jewels of power see a dragon soaring secretly
Over the lost lands of the six towns
The spell will blast them away, blowing
Like a feather in the wind.

She turned away and flew at a safe distance round the towering spikes of black rock enclosing Stoplar and its lands. She didn't see another pass during her long flight and her muscles ached as she neared the place she'd started from. *It's hopeless*, she thought, *there's definitely no other way through. We'll have to do what Finn suggested and let him fly me in.*

A tremendous groaning startled her into back-winging furiously. The storm ground to a halt with a great creaking and moaning, splinters of ice crashed to the ground, and the mists parted. Tia hovered in surprise as a line of people with horses and carts made their way out of the pass.

'Traders!' Tia scanned the faces of the people below and saw her special friends, Kizzy and Florian. They'd be amazed to see a small golden dragon flying above them – and even more amazed if they knew it was her.

She glided down. Kizzy spotted her and pointed, wide-eyed. Tia couldn't resist breathing fire. She only meant to show off a little, but a great stream of flames shot from her mouth. The terrified horses squealed and threw their riders or kicked at the traces of the carts.

Tia couldn't believe what she'd done – she'd acted like Torkil who enjoyed making trouble for the Traders. *But I didn't mean to do that*, she thought. *I'll change back and see if I can help.* She looked round for a place where she could turn into her own form without being seen and realised, too late, she'd flown into the spell.

It caught her by the tail and shook her until her wings crumpled. She tumbled helplessly away from the mountainside, over the foothills and towards the river. And then she was falling.

She'd reached the edge of the spell's power and it had dropped her but she was too exhausted to flap her wings and save herself. She plunged towards the river.

In desperation she gripped the opal with a scaly foot and thought – *fish!* She instantly changed into a salmon, twisting and turning as she hurtled to the river.

Splash! Salmon-Tia hit the water and was torn away by raging currents. Frantically she dodged the clashing ice floes streaming wildly along in the torrents of freezing water. Two floes closed in on either side and she leapt out of the water just as they crashed together. Down she came again, dodging jagged lumps of ice flashing by. She dived deep, right to the bottom of the river bed, and powered along with ice swirling above her.

She swam for what felt like miles before the current grew weaker and the floes moved more slowly. Then she drifted along until she reached shallow water. At last she changed back into herself, stumbled to the bank and fell to her knees, shivering violently.

A shadow fell over her. It was Finn, puffing out agitated little bursts of smoke. 'Are you all right?'

'I'm fine,' she said through chattering cold.' She wrapped her arms round herself and tried to stop shivering.

Finn grasped her in his claws and flew back to the campsite in the trees. While he flopped by the fire Tia changed into dry clothes. Neither her DragonBrother nor Loki said a word to her.

Chapter Three

Into Stoplar

The fire crackled and Tia felt warmth gradually returning to her bones. Steam rose from her clothes drying in front of the fire and she tugged her spare jacket tightly round herself. 'How did you find me?' she asked Finn and Loki.

'When we realised you'd gone we went to look for you. I saw you fall and change into the silver fish,' Finn said.

Loki shook his wings. 'You were easy to find – you were a very shiny dragon and you breathed a lot of fire.'

'I couldn't help the fire...' Tia was going to say that her dragon power of breathing fire had unexpectedly combined with her witch-power but realised she couldn't, not if she wanted to keep it a secret. Besides, she had been very, very foolish.

She sighed. 'I wanted to be a dragon so much.'

'I knew you'd use that opal,' the jackdaw said. He pecked Tia's hand sharply.

'Ow! What was that for?' Tia rubbed her hand.

'To remind you not to be so stupid in the future.'

Tia hugged her throbbing hand and said nothing; she knew it served her right. 'I'm sorry,' she said. 'I really am.'

Finn swung his head round and looked at her steadily with his green eyes. 'If you mean it, give me the opal.'

Tia's hand flew protectively to the jewel. 'But I promise not to use it,' she said.

'You promised before. Do you really think you'll be able to resist it now you know what it's like to be a dragon?'

Finn understood her better than anyone and she knew he was right: she'd be constantly tempted by the opal. Slowly she unfastened the collar and handed it to her DragonBrother. With his claws he delicately unpicked the metal hooks holding the jewel in its setting, threw the collar away into the trees and wrapped the opal in leaves.

'Give me your book bag,' he said.

Tia fetched the little green and silver sack and gave it to him. He dropped the opal inside. 'Have you still got that ball of leather strips from Kulafoss?' he asked. When Tia nodded he asked her to tie the strips to the bag and then loop them round his neck. Once she'd finished, the sack lay snugly against his throat.

'I need to keep the emerald,' Tia said, 'so I can talk to Loki and send him with messages.'

'Oh, that's right,' the jackdaw said. 'Loki do this, Loki do that and never mind the danger.'

Tia stroked his ruffled feathers. 'You know how important you are – we couldn't have stolen the emerald or the opal without you,' she said. 'And Finn lets you ride him.'

She grinned at her DragonBrother. 'You could let me ride you over the mountains into Stoplar.'

'Never!' The little dragon's eyes glittered in the firelight. 'I'll carry you – be ready just before dawn. And this time don't go missing.'

'I won't,' Tia said meekly.

It was freezing in the dark spring morning and it grew steadily colder as Finn flew higher and higher

over the mountains through buffeting winds and
flurries of snow. Just as Tia thought she was going
to freeze to death Finn began to fly downwards to
where the air grew warm and the howling wind
changed to a gentle breeze.

They landed on the edge of a huge circular plain that they could easily make out in the fading moonlight. 'What a strange place,' Tia whispered.

Loki hopped from Finn's shoulder. 'The sun's going to rise soon – he'd better go,' the jackdaw said to Tia.

She hugged Finn and he breathed smoke over her. 'Be careful,' he warned.

'I will.'

The gust of air from Finn's take-off blew into her eyes and she shielded them with a hand while she watched him fly up into the mountains.

When he'd gone Loki cocked his head to one side and said, 'It's odd you can see him when no-one else can.'

Tia didn't want to tell the clever jackdaw it was because of her witch powers. 'I suppose it's because I know him so well,' she said.

'Hmm.' Loki didn't sound convinced. He flew into a tree growing nearby and hid amongst its leaves. Tia settled with her back against the tree meaning to watch the sun rise. Gradually she fell asleep in the balmy, sweet-smelling air.

She dreamt she was back in the Drakelow Mountains, in the teaching cave. DragonTeacher watched as she wrote runes in the sandy floor of the cave with a metal claw that fitted over her finger. Freya, her DragonMother, had asked the Traders to make it especially for her.

'No, no, no!' DragonTeacher said and swept away the shaky runes with his tail. 'Try again!'

'Stupid witch-brat!' a dragonet sniggered. The others joined in and their chanting grew louder, their voices echoing round the cave – *witch-brat, witch-brat, witch-brat.*

With a start Tia woke up. It was daylight. Sunshine warmed her face and the voices of children rang in her ears.

Chapter Four

The Saffron Fields

Tia stood up and stared in amazement. Stoplar lay in a sun-drenched bowl scooped out of the snow-covered black mountains towering around it. In the centre lay a vast stretch of rich brown earth tilled into low ridges. This was patrolled by children who waved and called to each other as they passed. Several also walked around a wall that divided the plain from slopes of lush grass dotted with plump sheep and small black cows.

Here and there stood farms, and behind them, reaching right to the boundary of the mountains, were orchards of apples, pears, cherries and other trees Tia didn't recognise.

On the far side of the bowl was the town. It was as strange and beautiful as the rest of this sunny land in the middle of the cold mountains. Brightly painted houses filled rows of terraces that rose in steps up the steep foothills, while above them was a shining white building with hundreds of windows. It was so dazzling in the sunshine that Tia had to shade her eyes.

As she squinted through laced fingers she thought, *It must be Luona's castle but it's more like a palace – there aren't any fortifications or gates.* Tia supposed the High Witch felt protected by the ice-storm blocking the pass; her enemies would never be able to get through it.

Someone called out from quite close. It was a boy of about Tia's own age. He was glaring at an enormous, long-haired white cat scratching at the soil, scattering it in all directions.

The boy shouted and threw a lump of earth towards the cat. It fell well short and the animal ignored him.

Tia grinned. She climbed on top of the wall, took her sling and a pebble out of her pocket, whirled it around her head and pitched the stone towards the cat. It landed – thud – just in front of the cat's nose and the creature leapt straight up in the air with a screech of fright. It glared at Tia then ran away in a blur of white.

The boy stared at Tia as she wound up her sling, jumped down from the wall and walked up to him.

'You nearly hit the Lady Luona's cat!' he said.

'I wouldn't hit it,' she said indignantly. 'I don't hurt animals – I just scared it off. Isn't that what you were trying to do?'

'Of course, it's part of my job. But who are you, Trader girl? And what are you doing here? Your people left yesterday.'

Tia told her familiar story. 'I'm Nadya. I fell asleep and got left behind.' She thought of another detail. 'I suppose my parents thought I was with my cousin, Florian.'

'What are you going to do? The Lady Luona won't open the pass just so the Traders can come back for you.'

'I don't know. I suppose I could find work.'

The boy laughed. 'You don't know much about Stoplar, do you? You can't have a job unless you get a work badge.'

'How do I do that?' Tia asked. She'd never heard of such a thing.

'You need to go to the Great Palace and register as an Outsider.'

'I'll go now.' Tia hefted her bag and started to trudge across the plain.

'Be careful!' The boy ran after her, jumping over the ridges as he went. 'Don't disturb the saffron bulbs – they're near to blossoming.'

Tia thought furiously, trying to remember her lessons on the history of Tulay. What had DragonTeacher said about the precious spice that grew only in Stoplar? That the saffron flowers bloomed just once a year and had to be gathered quickly before they withered away.

She looked at the folds of brown soil. There wasn't even a hint of green shoots anywhere.

'How d'you know they're going to flower soon?' she asked.

He shrugged. 'It's always that way. They just suddenly appear.' He glared at her. '*If* you don't disturb the bulbs, that is – you're as bad as the cats.'

'I'll be careful,' she promised and lifted her leg high to take an exaggerated step over the nearest ridge.

The boy laughed. 'Wait, you'll need somewhere to stay if you're going to register for work. Go to my mother first, her name's Jofranka and she lives in the green house on Brekka Street.'

'Jofranka – that's a Trader name!' Tia said.

'Yes, she settled in a house with my father. As you're a Trader too I know she'll want to look after you. Tell her I sent you – my name's Yonas.'

Tia thanked him and set off again. Striding carefully over each ridge meant she couldn't walk quickly and it took her a long time to reach the other side of the plain.

The sun was high in the sky by the time she reached a gate leading onto a road running round the first terrace. She stopped a man in fine clothes and asked him the way to Brekka Street.

He looked her up and down suspiciously. 'What are you doing here, Trader girl?' he asked.

Tia recited her story and said she was looking for Jofranka.

The man sniffed haughtily and told her that Brekka Street was on the third level. She thanked him, even though she wanted to stick her tongue out at his rudeness, and ran off to find the green house. A plump Trader woman answered her knock. Tia explained that Yonas had sent her and why.

Jofranka opened the door wider. 'Come in child,' she said. In no time at all Tia was sitting at a well-scrubbed wooden table groaning with food. She ate while Jofranka asked questions about 'Nadya's' family. Tia was glad to be eating – it gave her time to think of believable answers to the Trader woman's sharp questions. She must've been satisfied because when Tia could eat no more Jofranka beamed, wrapped a sweet pie in a checked cloth, put it in a basket and said, 'Up you get, child.'

'Where are we going?' Tia asked as Jofranka bustled them both out into the street.

'To the Great Palace to get you a work badge. Only citizens are allowed to work here without one – outsiders have to be given special permission.'

'Why?'

'The Lady Luona likes it that way.' Jofranka stopped and caught Tia's arm. 'You know little of our customs here which is strange for a Trader,' she said in the language of her people.

'I'm always getting told off for daydreaming,' Tia said in the same language. 'I should've listened more carefully.'

Jofranka let go of her arm and looked thoughtfully at her. 'When we arrive at the palace, let me do the talking and follow what I say.'

Tia nodded, glad that she'd paid attention when her Trader friends had taught her their language and described the towns of Tulay.

Chapter Five

The Work Badge

Tia gazed in awe at the palace. She touched the pure white stone covering its walls. 'What is this?' she asked.

'Marble, from the quarries of Iserborg,' Jofranka told her and walked on, past the grand entrance of the palace guarded by two soldiers, to the far end where she turned into a narrow street running down the side. The further they went, the narrower and darker it grew. The marble facing on the walls abruptly came to an end revealing crudely cut blocks of black rock. The white stone was just for show.

Eventually Jofranka stopped at a mean-looking doorway with a grille set into it. She knocked at the door and the grille slid open. A grim-faced man peered out.

'What?'

'I've come to apply for a work badge for my niece. She was accidentally left behind yesterday when the Traders moved on,' Jofranka said.

Tia almost let out a gasp of surprise. She hadn't expected the Trader woman to pretend to be her aunt.

The grille slammed shut with a bang and the door opened. The sour man jerked his head. 'In,' he ordered.

His room was dark and musty; the only warmth came from a fire crackling in a tiny hearth. The man shuffled to a large desk piled high with papers and shooed away a streaky grey and white cat with a flat face and spiteful blue eyes. It stalked to a sack in front of the fire, curled up and glared.

'Now,' the man said, 'you want a work badge.' He sucked his teeth and shook his head. 'We have all the Outsiders we need.'

'I'd be very grateful if you could give my niece a badge,' Jofranka said.

'How grateful?'

Jofranka took out the sweet pie and put it on his desk.

'And?' the man said.

The Trader woman held out her hand. Two silver marks lay in it. The man grunted. Jofranka added a

third mark. The man snatched them and dropped them into a drawer. 'Name of Outsider?' he said.

'Nadya, niece of Jofranka of Brekka Street,' the Trader said.

He stamped a piece of paper and gave it to her.

'And the badge?' she asked.

He rummaged in another drawer and pulled out a square yellow and purple badge which he pushed across the desk to Tia. 'Don't lose it – you're not getting another one.'

'I won't.' Tia carefully pinned the badge to her jacket.

The man waved them away and started eating his pie.

Outside again they hurried back to the main street and the warm bright sun.

'I'll give you back the marks when I get paid,' Tia said.

Jofranka smiled. 'In good time – for now let me show you round Stoplar.'

Stoplar was a colourful town: as well as the brightly painted houses the terrace edges had flower-studded creepers draped over them like vividly dyed carpets. Jofranka led Tia up and down flights of steps linking the terraces and streets until she was familiar with the town.

The street on the lowest terrace was filled with shops, inns, eating houses and markets covered with striped awnings. They stopped at a market stall piled high with foodstuffs and the Trader woman greeted a large, cheerful-looking man.

'Hawkon, our son's sent us a guest. This is Nadya who was accidentally left behind by the Traders yesterday.'

'That will never do,' Hawkon boomed. 'We can look after you till your people return.'

'I've got a work badge,' Tia said quickly. 'I can earn my keep.'

Jofranka patted Tia's shoulder. 'Why don't you go and look round the market while I talk to Hawkon,' she suggested.

'All right,' Tia agreed, giving them a big, beaming smile before she wandered off. She knew that they wanted to talk about her, and as soon as she was out of sight she doubled back and crouched down behind Hawkon's stall where she couldn't be seen.

'I'm not sure you should've lied about Nadya being your niece,' she heard Hawkon say.

'Claiming she was a relative was the only way to get her a work badge, you know that. Even then I had to use bribes.'

'Oh well, it's done now. And I'm sure she won't have any problem working in the fields with the other children,' Hawkon said.

'That's what I thought – and now I'd better find her. Yonas will be back home soon.'

Tia quickly crept backwards and then strolled round to the other side of the stall.

'Ah, there you are,' Jofranka said. It's time for us go and for Hawkon to lock up the stall for the night.'

They waved goodbye and went back to the green house where Jofranka showed Tia to a simple, white-painted room on the ground floor. She opened the lid of a large chest, gathered up an armful of blankets and dropped them onto a couch underneath a small window overlooking the garden.

'You can store your bag in the chest and make up a bed while I prepare our meal.' She bustled away and Tia arranged the bedding on the couch.

Tap, tap, tap. Someone was rapping on the window pane.

Tia looked up in surprise to see Loki perched on the windowsill. He rapped again, impatiently.

As she scrambled onto the couch and opened the window Tia thought how strange it was that such an ordinary house had real glass in its windows. Usually only palaces and castles had glass panes. The people of Stoplar must be wealthy.

Loki flew in and landed on top of the chest. 'I've had a busy day following you around,' he said. 'What've you learned from the boy and the Trader woman?'

She told him and then asked if he'd found out anything useful about Stoplar.

'It's full of cats. The white ones are the worst – I've had a few narrow escapes while I've been trailing after you instead of paying attention to my own safety.'

Tia got out a piece of pie crust that she'd put in her pocket for the jackdaw, crumbled it up and spread the pieces on the chest. 'You should look after yourself first,' she told him.

He was too busy pecking at the crust to reply and when Jofranka called Tia for a meal she left him eating the last of the crumbs.

Chapter Six

Purple and Gold

The evening was a very jolly one. Hawkon roared with laughter at his own jokes and Yonas encouraged him while Jofranka teased them both. Tia enjoyed being part of a family; she missed curling up with Finn and Freya in their cave in the Drakelow Mountains, watching firelight dancing on the walls and listening to Freya tell tales of mighty dragons and their deeds.

But if Tia was to steal back the magic topaz she needed to know more about Stoplar, and especially Luona.

So while Hawkon drew breath between jokes, Tia asked Yonas what she would have to do in the saffron fields.

'Patrol the plain to make sure the bulbs don't get eaten by mice or bugs and slugs, and check the wall around the plain. If animals get in they trample on the ridges and crush the bulbs.'

'What about the cats?'

'We try to keep them out too but they get in to hunt the mice and scratch up the soil.'

'Are they all Luona's?' Tia asked.

'The *Lady* Luona's cats are the pure white ones. No-one else is allowed to keep those.' Yonas yawned. 'We ought to get some sleep now – we have to start at sunrise.'

Tia was tired too – she'd started her day even before Yonas – and was glad to go to bed. When she got to her room she told Loki about the work she'd have to do.

'That sounds dull,' the jackdaw said.

Tia agreed but they were both wrong; the next day turned out to be quite different from the one Yonas had described – and a lot more exciting.

Overnight the plain had been transformed into a sea of purple crocuses and people were everywhere, going up and down the ridges, stooping to pick the flowers.

Tia stared in astonishment. 'But there were no flowers yesterday!'

Yonas laughed. 'I told you, they just suddenly appear.'

'And who are all these people? Where have they come from?'

'Some are from the farms or the town but mostly they're Outsiders from the sorting sheds.' Yonas tugged at Tia's sleeve. 'C'mon. No time for talking – the really hard work starts now.'

He grabbed a couple of baskets from a huge pile by the wall and led Tia to the nearest ridge. He bent down, carefully pulled out one of the purple crocuses and laid it in the basket. 'You do it like that. Don't squash the petals or you'll ruin the saffron threads inside.'

Tia looked at her basket. It was very big and the flowers were very small – it was going to take a long time to fill. She bent down and started picking. As she pulled the first flower out of the ground a smell of honey and warm hay wafted up from the three red threads inside.

This is easy, she thought but by the end of an hour she was beginning to ache all over from the constant stooping. She glanced at the other pickers. They were working steadily. She bent to her task again and didn't stop till her basket was full. Then she straightened up and stretched. Yonas was also standing up; he'd finished at the same time. He grinned. 'Bet you're glad you've done your first basket.'

First! How many was she expected to fill in a day?

'We can have a walk now.' Yonas pointed to a dense stand of apple trees. 'The nearest sorting shed's behind those trees.'

'What are sorting sheds?' Tia asked as they set off.

'It's where the threads are sorted from the flower and dried in ovens to make the spice.'

'But you said that's where the Outsiders live.'

'They do. There's living lofts over the sorting area and they stay there till the harvest's done.'

'Then what happens?'

'The Lady Luona opens the pass and they leave.'

'Where do they go?'

Yonas shrugged uncomfortably. 'I don't know. Stop asking so many questions.'

He quickly climbed over the wall and hurried off. Tia wondered why her questions had annoyed him.

When they reached the trees Yonas reached up into an apple tree and pulled down a branch so they could pick the fruit.

Tia tugged off an apple and risked another question. 'How long does the harvest last?'

'Only twenty days.'

'Twenty days! I won't have any back left at the end of it!'

Yonas laughed. 'You'll get used to it. Here we are.'

The ugly, long, two-storey building was well hidden by trees. Tia thought they looked as if they'd been planted on purpose to hide the grubby painted walls and the roof full of holes patched with branches and leaves. The windows running all down one side of the ground floor were filled with precious glass but it was cracked and dirty.

Yonas and Tia went inside. Three long tables stretched from end to end of the room with rows of people sitting at them on benches; each person had a pile of purple flowers in front of them and a small bowl. They were carefully opening the flowers, pulling out the three red threads and dropping them into the bowls. They did this in silence as a man and woman walked up and down inspecting the work. At each end of the room an open clay oven smouldered with fire-rock, making the air hot and oppressive.

Tia and Yonas gently tipped their flowers onto an empty table at the top of the room then left quickly. Tia was glad to be outside again. She sat on the bottom step of a flight of stairs running up to a door on the upper storey and took deep breaths of fresh air.

The door jerked open and an Outsider woman in shabby clothes came hurrying down. Tia stood up to let her pass but the woman banged into her and she went sprawling on the grass.

'I'm sorry,' the woman said. She pulled Tia up, brushed grass and leaves from her jacket, apologised again, then rushed away and disappeared among the trees. Tia and Yonas looked at each other, startled; it had happened so quickly and the woman had behaved so strangely.

Are you all right?' Yonas asked.

'Yes, just surprised.'

'Off to the fields, then,' Yonas said.

With a groan Tia picked up her basket and followed him to the plain.

Chapter Seven

Luona the High Witch

Back in the fields they saw the strange Outsider woman picking saffron flowers. Tia and Yonas decided to ignore her and work in a different area. At noon Jofranka brought them a meal and some news.

'The Lady Luona is coming to see how work is progressing,' she told them as they climbed up on the wall and began eating.

Tia munched her pie thoughtfully. She was going to see her third High Witch aunt. Would she be beautiful like Malindra or ugly like Yordis? Whichever it was, she was certain to be just as cruel and dangerous as they were.

'Do you know when she'll be here?' she asked.

Jofranka shook her head. 'She'll come when she's ready.'

They three of them chattered away until the food was eaten, then Jofranka waved goodbye and Tia and Yonas went back to work. As Tia leaned down to start picking a small dark shape flew over her head and landed on the wall where they'd been sitting. It was Loki. He pecked at the crumbs they'd left behind. Tia hoped he was keeping one eye open for the white cats.

Luona didn't arrive till Tia had filled three more baskets and delivered them to the sorting shed.

The High Witch, accompanied by her women and surrounded by guards, walked haughtily along a stone-flagged path running round the field. Everyone bowed as she passed.

She was tall and slender and her pale blonde hair, decorated with plumes and glittering stones, was piled high, making her look taller still. She wore a white gown and an orange-yellow sash fastened by a buckle set with a large, deep yellow jewel. She stroked it and, just for a moment, Tia saw a shimmer of enchantment around it. The magic topaz!

Curious to see it more clearly, Tia made her way closer to the little procession. She'd almost drawn level with Luona when a hand fell on her shoulder.

'What d'you think you're doing?' a harsh voice demanded. It was one of Luona's guards. He shook Tia so hard that her teeth rattled and she couldn't answer.

'Where's your work badge?' He peered at her suspiciously.

'It's here.' She pointed at her jacket – but the badge was gone.

Tia looked round wildly for help. The Outsider woman who'd banged into her glanced away furtively and put her hand over the badge pinned to her dress. Tia was sure that the woman had pushed her over deliberately and stolen her badge.

'Unauthorised Outsider brat – it's the ice prison for you!' The guard started shaking her again.

'Stop!' A blast of freezing wind wrapped itself round them. The guard instantly let go of Tia and dropped on one knee, head down.

The High Witch beckoned. 'Come here girl.'

Tia hurried forward, heart beating fast.

Luona gripped her chin, forcing her to look up. She examined Tia's face, turning it this way and that.

'Hmm.' Luona let go of Tia and gestured to one of her women. 'Asta, take the child to the palace. Put her in a lesser guest room and keep watch until I send for her.'

'Yes, Lady,' Asta said.

Without another word Luona swung round and she and her procession swept on.

'My, but that was a close escape!' Asta said. 'It was lucky that my Lady Luona took a liking to you.'

The woman chatted all the way to the palace; the only thing she asked Tia was her name and how she came to be in Stoplar.

They went through the imposing entrance, into marble halls, up stairs carpeted with crimson and into a grand chamber where a white cat lounged on a bed spread with fine coverings. Asta pushed it off and tutted at the scattered hairs it left behind.

The cat hissed at her as it slunk out, and snarled, 'If you touch me again I'll give you a good scratching!'

Horrible animal! It's a shame I can't tell it off, Tia thought.

She bounced on the bed and stared around. If this was a lesser guest room she couldn't imagine how grand the others were. The walls were hung with tapestries showing the seasons of the year and the windows were draped with curtains embroidered all over with saffron flowers. The floor was cool white marble dotted with yellow rugs.

Asta opened a door to one side. 'This is the bathing room. You need to be clean when the High Witch summons you. I'll bring you fresh clothes.'

Why did people always want to change her clothes? Tia wondered.

'And you can get bathed while I go – you're all sweaty.' Asta shook her head in disapproval and went out locking the door behind her.

You'd be sweaty if you'd been picking flowers in the hot sun all day! Tia thought indignantly. She rubbed her aching back. Perhaps plunging into hot water would be a good idea after all.

After her bath she found Asta waiting with a simple tunic and long skirt.

'I have to wait on the Lady Luona. I've put a meal for you on the table by the window. Get changed before you eat and be ready for when she wants to see you.'

Tia nodded. As soon as Asta had gone she dressed in the tunic and skirt and went to the table. She looked out of the window as she ate; down on the plain the saffron pickers were still toiling away in the last of the daylight.

She opened the window and scanned the darkening sky. A small black bird with a grey head was flying slowly round the palace. It had to be Loki. She waved furiously. He saw her and flew in through the window, landing with a bounce and a hop on the table.

'I see you've got yourself captured again,' he said.

'It wasn't my fault!' Tia explained about the Outsider woman and the badge and Luona's sudden, unexpected interest in her. 'I don't know why she wants to see me but at least now I'm in the palace I can find out more about the topaz and plan how to steal it back.'

A key rattled in the lock.

'It's Asta! Hide!' Tia whispered and Loki flew behind a curtain.

Asta poked her head round the door. 'Come on, girl – the Lady Luona wants to see you now and she doesn't like to be kept waiting.'

Tia hurried out. What could the High Witch want with her?

Chapter Eight

Loki in Trouble

Luona was in a grand chamber sitting on a grand chair, carved with gilded symbols of the wind and sun, clouds and snow crystals.

She pointed to a padded stool at her feet. 'Sit here, child,' she said sternly, 'and look at me.'

Tia obediently sat down and looked up at the High Witch.

'Asta told me your name is Nadya and you live with Traders.'

'Yes, Lady,' Tia lied. 'My parents died in a storm and the Traders took me in.'

'You were fortunate.' The High Witch leaned forward and stroked Tia's hair. 'You remind me of my sister, Ondine. She has hair of the same colour.'

Tia sat very still. She was suddenly afraid. Surely Luona couldn't suspect her true identity?

'Since we High Witches became rulers of all Tulay, we have been confined to our own lands and do not see each other.' Luona sighed. 'I miss my little sister.'

She smiled suddenly, all her grim sadness gone. 'You shall take her place and live in the palace with me.'

Before Tia knew what was happening Luona had summoned Asta, told her to bring Tia fine clothes, look after her and instruct her in the ways of the palace. Then, just as abruptly, she waved them out.

Asta laughed at Tia's expression. 'She's as changeable as the wind! She'll make a fuss of you for a few days then probably forget about you once she starts bartering with the spice merchants. When she's done with that she'll send for you again – until something else catches her attention.'

That suited Tia. She didn't want Luona's attention. And she could explore the castle and find out about the topaz while Luona was busy. 'Who are the spice merchants?' she asked Asta as they walked back to the guest chamber.

'They come every year to buy our saffron. It's the finest in the world,' Asta boasted, 'and it's very valuable – even more costly than gold. That's why Stoplar is so rich.'

'The Outsiders don't look rich,' Tia said, thinking about their shabby clothes and the bare, rickety sorting sheds they lived in.

'They don't belong to Stoplar – they're from poor villages beyond the pass. They come here to work at harvest time. They'll do anything to get a work badge and earn money picking the flowers.'

Even stealing, Tia thought. The Outsider woman who'd taken her badge had probably lost her own and was scared she'd be sent away or punished.

'Why don't they move to Stoplar? Then they could work all the year round.'

'They did live here once,' Asta admitted. 'But the Lady Luona banished them when she used the topaz to change the weather and favour the saffron harvest. There's only enough work for them now at harvest time.'

'Couldn't they do different work during the rest of the year?'

Asta had stopped smiling. She looked as uncomfortable as Yonas had at the questions about the Outsiders. 'They used to tend their land but the High Witch took it for the bulbs. There isn't enough other work to go round.'

As they neared the chamber Asta changed the subject. 'I'll bring you finer clothes...'

Tia sighed. 'Do I have to wear them?'

Asta laughed. 'Only when the Lady Luona summons you.'

Tia brightened and Asta laughed again. 'In the morning I'll show you around the palace and teach you how to behave.'

Suddenly a terrible squawking and mewling burst from inside the chamber.

'What's that?' Asta said.

Tia knew. It was Loki shrieking in alarm and a cat sneering, 'Make as much noise as you like, jackdaw, no-one's coming to help you.'

Asta and Tia burst into the room. Black and grey feathers and clumps of white fur swirled in the air as Loki fought off two enormous white cats trying to pin him to the floor. They turned their flat faces and snarled.

'You don't frighten me,' Tia shouted. 'Get off that bird!'

The cats hissed in surprise. 'You can speak to us!' one said.

'I'll do more than yell at you if you don't let the jackdaw go,' Tia said, hoping Asta didn't realise she was actually talking to the cats. She kicked out at them, making sure she missed but coming close enough to give them a fright.

They leaped away from Loki. He flew to the top of a curtain yakking furiously as the cats stalked out.

Tia banged the door shut. She could hear the cats muttering evilly on the other side. 'Horrible animals!'

Asta opened the window. 'I hope the poor bird will be able to fly away. He can't stay here all night.'

'It's dark now – he won't fly at night. I don't mind if he stays till morning.'

'All right then, if you're sure.' Asta closed the window, drew the curtains and turned down the bed. 'Goodnight, Nadya.'

As soon as she was gone, Loki flew down and Tia made a big fuss of him, stroking his feathers and telling him how brave he was and how well he'd fought the cats.

'But how did they get in?' she wondered.

'When you left, a servant came in to clear up your dinner things and the cats must've followed him. I didn't see them till it was too late.' Loki shook his wings and shuddered.

'We'll both have to take care now they know I can speak to animals and birds,' Tia said. 'They're bound to tell the other cats and cause problems for us.'

'I'm not going to let them catch me out again,' Loki said. He flew back to the top of the curtain, put his head under his wing and went to sleep.

Tia got ready for the night too. Once she was in bed she took out the locket that hung on her chain next to the emerald. She opened it and looked at the picture of her father, Elio. He'd promised to come and rescue her from the dragons when they stole her away but she'd never seen him since. It was all the High Witches' fault.

She thought about how Luona had seen a resemblance between her and Ondine. For a moment she was tempted to pull off the paper covering her mother's picture in the other half of the locket, just to see, but then she snapped it shut. Tia didn't want to be like her mother.

She turned down the oil lamp and wriggled deeper into the soft bed. Even though it was warm and cosy, Tia preferred her bracken-strewn shelf in Freya's cavern. She was a true DragonChild, nothing like the High Witches. And when she'd returned all the jewels of power, everyone would know it.

She drifted off to sleep, more determined than ever to find the topaz as soon as she could.

Chapter Nine

The Ice Prison

Just as Asta had said, Luona made a fuss of Tia for the next few days: she moved her to a grand chamber near her own and took her everywhere she went.

'It's very annoying,' Tia grumbled to Loki one morning. 'I haven't had a chance to explore the castle. If I try to creep out at night there's always one of her cats waiting to follow me, mewing and screeching. I can't do anything in secret.'

'What about the topaz? Have you seen where she keeps it when she's not wearing it?'

Tia nodded. 'It's in a metal cabinet set in the wall of her sleeping area. It's sealed with a magical lock that you have to press in a special pattern.'

'Have you worked it out?'

'Not yet, but I will.'

Tia wished she felt as confident as she sounded. She jumped up. 'Now I've got to get ready for a grand midday meal. The spice merchants have arrived to trade for saffron and Luona wants to show me off like one of her pet cats.'

Loki huffed at the mention of the cats.

Tia opened a cupboard door and scowled at the clothes inside. 'What shall I wear, Loki?'

'*I* don't know,' the jackdaw said. 'I'm content with my feathers.'

'They're all dresses – they won't hide my chain and Luona will see the emerald. I'll have to take it off.' She unclasped the chain and slid the emerald ring into her palm. 'Where can I put it?'

'I'll guard it for you,' Loki said.

'Keep it somewhere safe,' Tia said, holding it out.

He took it and stood with one foot on the jewel so that he could speak to her. 'I'll hide it in an old chimney where even the cats can't go.'

'You don't need to take it away,' Tia said.

'It'll be safer,' Loki insisted and flew out of the window. Tia felt uneasy without the emerald, but there was nothing she could do. She re-fastened her chain and turned back to the cupboard, wishing she could fly away with her jackdaw friend instead of dressing up for the High Witch.

The meal was very grand indeed and so were the spice merchants. Tia had never seen such silks and satins, waving plumes and glittering jewels.

'What do you think to my guests, Nadya?' Luona asked.

Tia thought many of them looked cruel with their darting, suspicious eyes and dishonest smiles. 'They're very... splendid, Lady,' she said hoping she sounded truthful. 'Though not as splendid as you.'

Luona smiled and patted Tia's hand. 'You are an observant child.'

She turned abruptly to a small, thin woman on her other side and began talking to her as though Tia had disappeared. Tia didn't mind; it gave her a chance to listen to their conversation without them noticing.

A spice merchant leaned towards the High Witch. 'Lady, have you not heard that the emerald and the opal have been stolen?'

'What?' Luona's fist crashed to the table and the sky outside grew dark.

The room fell silent, all eyes on Luona and the merchant. Tia tried to make herself look small and innocent.

'Malindra and Yordis have been captured,' the merchant went on. 'Their people have rebelled and they are both imprisoned in their own castles.'

Thunder exploded and black clouds churned over the palace. 'Who has dared do such a thing?' Luona shrieked and gripped the topaz protectively.

Tia slid from her chair and began to back quietly away.

'It was all the work of a mysterious Trader child,' the merchant said. 'They say her name is Nadya.'

'No!' Luona cried and the storm clouds broke.

Tia ran for the door, desperately dodging this way and that. It was no use; hands snatched at her, and dragged her to the High Witch.

Lightning darted and flared, reflected in Luona's eyes. 'Take this creature to her chamber and wait for me,' she seethed.

Tia was hauled away past the sneering merchants. She was a captive with no-one to help her, not even Loki.

Luona ransacked Tia's room looking for the emerald and the opal. Tia was thankful that Loki had taken the ring.

'Where are the jewels?' Luona demanded.

'I don't know,' Tia said truthfully. 'I haven't got them, really I haven't.'

'Liar!' Luona raged. Outside lightning split the dark sky, and thunder boomed in the gathering storm.

'The harvest, Lady!' Asta said. 'The saffron will be ruined!'

'Do you think I care? This, this... *deceiver* has stolen my sisters' jewels and refuses to give them to me!'

'I can't give you them!' Tia shouted. 'I don't know where they are!' She tried frantically to think of a way to convince Luona that it was all a terrible mistake.

Luona shook with fury and torrents of water crashed against the windows. 'Why did I think you resembled my beloved sister? She would never have betrayed me as you have done.'

That stung Tia – saying she was worse than her thieving mother! It was too much for her to ignore. 'You betrayed the dragons when you stole their jewels!' she shouted at Luona.

The wind howled and battered against the windows till the glass bulged under the strain.

'Please, Lady!' Asta fell to her knees. 'You will destroy Stoplar. You will lose everything.'

Luona closed her eyes, breathed a juddering breath in and a slow, calm one out. She stroked the topaz gently and the storm subsided. She opened her eyes again.

'Asta, put this, this *robber* back in her Trader rags. My guards will parade her through the streets so all my people will see exactly what she is – a common thief. She is to be taken to the ice prison and left there as an example to all who would disobey me.'

The High Witch swept out.

Asta brought Tia her Trader clothes and she changed silently while Asta stood by, her face cold.

There was a pounding at the door and two huge guards marched in.

Asta hastily stepped back and the guards took Tia away.

The march through Stoplar town that evening was terrible. Among the watching crowds was the Outsider woman who'd stolen Tia's badge. She was weeping. Further on, Tia saw Yonas between Hawkon and Jofranka; all three were white-faced. The rest of the walk to the ice prison passed in a blur.

When she reached it, at the bottom of the narrow lane made from black rock, Luona was waiting. She pointed to one of the tiny cells carved in the stone, coated with blue ice and jagged with icicles. The guards pushed Tia inside.

The High Witch grasped the topaz, waved her other hand and sealed the entrance with a sheet of clear ice.

For a while Luona watched Tia shivering, frost forming on her eyebrows and lashes, her breath coming in cloudy gasps. When she slid to the frozen floor Luona smiled and walked away.

Chapter Ten

Stealing the Topaz

As soon as she was sure the High Witch and her guards had gone, Tia sat up. She had pretended to be weaker than she was, in the hope that Luona would go away while she still had some strength. But she was afraid it was already too late – she was so cold! If she didn't get warm very soon she'd freeze to death. She tried to snap her fingers to make fire. They were too numb and she was shivering too much. She tried again and again. It was hopeless and she was so tired.

If I go to sleep, I'll never wake up, she thought. *But I need to rest, just for a moment...*

She sank back against the icy walls and felt a chill seeping deep inside her. Her eyelids drooped shut, her head fell forward and she began to drift off to sleep.

A dark shape beat against the sheet of ice. 'Tia! Wake up!' it called.

Tia's eyelids fluttered open and she saw Loki frantically flapping his wings against the ice. Something green glittered in his foot – the emerald.

'Tia – don't go back to sleep!'

With a rush of determination she lifted her frozen hand and breathed on her icy fingers. She tried to click them again. One tiny red spark flashed. Another click and more sparks flew. They warmed her fingertips just enough for her next click to be a strong one. Flames danced in her hand and warmth flooded back into her body.

'Move away, Loki,' she warned and snapped the fingers of both hands, hard.

A fierce spout of fire shot from them. The sheet of ice instantly melted into steam, and she stumbled through it into the road where Loki waited with the emerald ring.

Tia stroked his grey head. 'Thank you, Loki.'

'I wasn't going to let that witch and her cats beat us,' he said. 'And you will keep getting captured.'

Tia didn't mention that she'd had to rescue him from the cats.

'I suppose you want this ring back now?' the jackdaw said.

'Yes please.' She threaded it on her chain and tucked it under her shirt.

Loki fluttered onto her shoulder. 'I thought you were a strong witch,' he said. 'Now I've seen you make fire like that, I know for sure.'

'Please don't tell Finn,' Tia pleaded. 'He might not like me if he knew I truly am a witch-child.'

'He'll always like you, but I won't say anything. Though you'll have to tell him one day.'

Tia didn't want to think about that for now, although she knew Loki was right.

'You're the cleverest, bravest jackdaw there ever was,' she said instead.

'I know,' he said smugly.

'And now I need you to help me get the topaz from Luona.'

Loki's sharp black eyes shone. 'I was afraid you were going to say that.'

Tia made a small fire and warmed herself thoroughly while they made plans. She decided to get her bag first and they slipped through the night to Jofranka's house.

Tia crept into the garden and climbed into her room through the open window. Her bag was still in the chest. She took out her book and pen and wrote:

I'm going to steal the topaz and open the pass. If you join with the outsiders you can overpower Luona and be free, like the people in Drangur and Kulafoss.

I'll return the silver marks one day. Thank you.

Nadya.

She tore the page out and went into the kitchen. She left the message on the table then went back into the bedroom and climbed out of the window.

'Now for the next part of the plan,' she whispered to Loki and they made their way to the palace. Two soldiers stood on guard at the entrance. Tia fitted a pebble into her sling and let it fly.

Clang! The stone hit a soldier's helmet and he crouched, hand on sword.

'What was that?' the second guard said.

Tia flung another pebble, this one further away down the road. The soldiers spun round. Tia's third pebble had them running down the road waving their swords.

As soon as they disappeared from sight Tia and Loki sneaked into the palace and stole through shadowy corridors to Luona's chambers. Inside, the High Witch was deeply asleep in the bed chamber with a cat curled up at her feet.

Tia tiptoed to the metal cabinet and Loki glided to the top. 'Hurry,' he hissed, 'there isn't much time. It'll be daylight soon.'

'I don't know the right way to do it,' she hissed back.

'It doesn't matter – you're a witch, use magic!'

'It's not as simple as that!'

'Yes it is,' the jackdaw insisted. 'Trust your ability – and be quick about it.'

Tia glared at Loki then turned to the symbols and stared hard at them. Nothing happened. She went on staring; she concentrated so hard that prickles of sweat stood out on her forehead. Still nothing happened.

A noise from the bed behind her made her glance round; the cat was dreaming, its whiskers and paws twitching. It might wake at any moment. Tia turned quickly back to the symbols, determined not to let Luona and her cats defeat her.

'Show yourself!' she ordered softly but firmly. A wisp of magic flickered over one of the symbols. She pressed it and the faint glimmer danced to another symbol and then another. Guided by the magic, Tia pressed each one in turn. The door clicked and swung open. The buckle lay inside.

Tia snatched it up and ran out, Loki zooming

overhead, and almost trod on a white cat. It went back on its haunches and spat, 'But you're in the ice prison!'

'Not any more!' Tia said and pelted for the entrance leaping over cats that appeared from everywhere.

'Halt!' The guards were back on duty. She dodged past them, cats swarming after her down the steps, tripping up the guards.

She soon outran the cats as she raced down streets faintly lit by the dawn. She passed the green house in Brekka Street and saw Hawkon, holding her note, talking to a group of people gathered at the door. They watched in astonishment as she sped by.

At the end of the town she reached the entrance to the pass where the ice-storm raged and wailed. Skidding to a halt she held up the buckle, the topaz cradled in her palm. She felt its power and thought of sunshine, warmth, blue skies.

Gradually the wind dropped and the ice crystals melted away in the warm air. The storm had gone.

'Hey!'

It was the guards. Tia had meant to run into the pass and seal it behind her before they caught up with her but now she didn't have time, even though they'd stopped to stare in astonishment at the open pass.

'Where's the ice-storm gone?' one asked.

'Don't know,' the other said, 'but it's none of our business.' He pointed his sword towards Tia. 'We've got to get her back to the Lady Luona.' The men advanced.

Tia gripped the topaz and felt its magic flow into her. Who did these puny guards think they were? She could freeze them on the spot if she wanted to, or zap them with lightning. Furious, she held up the buckle, the topaz fizzing with power.

The soldiers skidded to a halt. Tia laughed at the fear in their eyes – and then stopped, horrified at herself.

What am I doing? she thought. She was no better than her aunts!

She lowered her arm just as Hawkon and his friends appeared, pointing excitedly at the pass.

'Be a good girl and come with us,' one of the guards wheedled.

Instead Tia gripped the topaz lightly and thought of wind. A spout of spinning air appeared in front of her and she sent it whirling towards the soldiers. It gathered them up, spun them onwards and dumped them in front of Hawkon and his friends who promptly overpowered them.

Stopping only to send the wind away and thrust the buckle into her pocket, Tia ran off down the pass with Loki soaring overhead. She sped between its towering, rocky walls until she burst out into the open on the other side of the mountain. She couldn't wait to see Finn and used the last of her breath to run to the copse by the river. And there was her DragonBrother, waiting patiently. Tia threw her arms round his snout.

He butted her gently and blew anxious smoke rings while she got her breath back. When she was breathing normally again he said, 'Tell me all about your adventures in Stoplar.'

Tia sat on the ground, leant against her DragonBrother and, with Loki interrupting every now and again, told him about Luona, her cats and the spice merchants who'd brought news of the stolen jewels of power. And she told him about how she'd been tempted to use the topaz to harm the soldiers.

She held out the buckle. 'It's too powerful for me – you take it.'

Finn unpicked it from its setting and sent the buckle flying over the trees and into the river. Tia wrapped the jewel in leaves and put it in the bag around his neck.

'I think we need to leave for Iserborg as soon as we can,' he said, 'before news about the topaz reaches High Witch Skadi.'

Tia agreed. 'Especially as Skadi will already know about the first two jewels being stolen.'

'Which one does she have?' Loki asked.

'The sapphire,' Tia said. 'She uses it to move anywhere she wants to. If she wasn't stuck in Iserborg she could even send herself from one side of Tulay to the other.'

'That would be useful,' Loki said. 'Though not as useful as flying.'

Tia said, 'Ha!' and slung her bag onto her back. 'Since I've got to walk, let's get going.'

The three friends set off – Tia, her DragonBrother and Loki the jackdaw – on the long journey to Iserborg where High Witch Skadi held the magic sapphire.

Can Tia and her friends meet the challenge of
the fourth adventure? Find out in

The Sapphire Quest

published by A & C Black
November 2013